# DRESS-BOT
## MODEL NO: 15731

GETTING DRESSED WAS NEVER SO EASY! DRESS-BOT STYLES YOUR OUTFITS FOR EVERY OCCASION!

# CLEAN-BOT
## MODEL NO: 12967

DIRTY DISHES? MESSY HOUSE? LIVE LIKE A PIG AND CLEAN-BOT WILL MAKE YOUR HOME SPARKLE!

# BOOK-BOT
## MODEL NO: 7372

TOO BUSY TO READ? LET BOOK-BOT R[...]
HEAR THE LATEST CLASSIC FROM SE[...]

# TEETH-BOT
## MODEL NO: 12087

NOW WITH FLOSSING! *

[...]SHING YOUR GNASHERS? LET TEETH-BOT [...]OUR SMILE DAZZLE YOUR FRIENDS!

For Fidelma and Tony – S.T.

For Hal & Ida – R.C.

First published in Great Britain in 2013 by Andersen Press Ltd.,
20 Vauxhall Bridge Road, London SW1V 2SA.
Published in Australia by Random House Australia Pty.,
Level 3, 100 Pacific Highway, North Sydney, NSW 2060.
Text copyright © Sean Taylor, 2013.
Illustration copyright © Ross Collins, 2013.
The rights of Sean Taylor and Ross Collins to be identified as
the author and illustrator of this work have been asserted by them
in accordance with the Copyright, Designs and Patents Act, 1988.
All rights reserved. Colour separated in Switzerland by
Photolitho AG, Zürich.
Printed and bound in Malaysia by Tien Wah Press.
Ross Collins has used concentrated watercolour, vinyl, colour
and pen on watercolour paper in this book.

10    9    8    7    6    5    4    3    2    1

British Library Cataloguing in Publication Data available.

ISBN 978 1 84939 628 8

My mum and dad are busy.
So just last night they said,
"We decided to buy these fantastic robots
to get you into bed."

I thought they must be joking.
But Dad switched the robots on.
Mum said, "They're the latest models.
What could *possibly* go wrong?"

Then Cook-bot made spaghetti.
I ate the lot off my plate.

Clean-bot did the washing-up.
Everything seemed just great.

Wash-bot ran a bath.

It said, "YOU WILL BE SPICK AND SPAN."

I got my bath toys down off the shelf.

But that's when the rumpus began.

Crocodile is my favourite toy.
His teeth can really snap.
But soon as Wash-bot spotted him,
it got in a bit of a flap.

It said, "DANGEROUS ANIMAL IN THE WATER!"

Three warning-lights flashed red.

Then it went and slipped into Dress-bot,

who sat down on Teeth-bot's head.

Dress-bot turned round and round
like it didn't know what to do.

And Teeth-bot started brushing its head
and squirting toothpaste down the loo.

Clean-bot was whizzing about.
It was trying to keep things tidy.

But Dress-bot started putting pyjamas on the robot that had to dry me.

Cook-bot came in and stared.
And its warning-lights flashed too.
Then it nodded and zoomed away
like it knew just what to do.

I hoped it could sort out the mess.
This was getting beyond a laugh.
But all it did was cook more spaghetti
and tip it into the bath.

I **know** that robots can't cry,
But Clean-bot looked close to tears.

Book-bot sat with a book on the bed,
and smoke coming out its ears.

And Dry-bot couldn't manage to get my pyjamas off its head.

So, in the end, I left them
and got **myself** into bed.

I think the robots were exhausted.
They crashed around some more.
Then everything went quiet until . . .

The place was a bit of a mess.
It hadn't worked quite like they'd said.
And I don't think they got a good night's sleep . . .

AAAARGH!!!!

# With SEVEN ROBOTS IN THEIR BED!

# SCHOTT'S ROBOTS

*Be Overjoyed with a Droid!*

## SPRING CATALOGUE

DON'T DELAY! ORDER TODAY!
☎ PHONE 0800 932 ROBOT

## COOK-BOT
MODEL NO: 15642

EAT!

WITHDRAWN FOR TECHNICAL REASONS

YOU'LL NEVER DINE OUT AGAIN! WITH A COOK-BOT DELICIOUS MEALS FOR ALL! PASTA A SPECIALITY!

## WASH-BOT
MODEL NO: 13986

WASH!

WITHDRAWN FOR TECHNICAL REASONS

TOO LAZY TO WASH? LET WASH-BOT SPONGE OFF YOUR FILTH & ALWAYS SMELL LIKE ROSES!

## DRY-BOT
MODEL NO: 13278

WITHDRAWN FOR TECHNICAL REASONS

LATEST MODEL!

IS TOWELLING YOURSELF A CHORE? LET DRY-BOT GENTLY BLOW THE DAMP FROM YOUR SKIN!